HOPSC
TWISTY TA

Brownilocks
and the
Three Bowls of Cornflakes

by Enid Richemont and Polona Lovšin

W
FRANKLIN WATTS
LONDON•SYDNEY

This story is based on the traditional fairy tale,
Goldilocks and the Three Bears, but with a
new twist. You can read the original story
in Hopscotch Fairy Tales. Can you
make up your own twisty tale?

First published in 2010 by
Franklin Watts
338 Euston Road
London
NW1 3BH

Franklin Watts Australia
Level 17/207 Kent Street
Sydney
NSW 2000

Text © Enid Richemont 2010
Illustrations © Polona Lovšin 2010

The rights of Enid Richmont to be identified as the author
and Polona Lovšin as the illustrator of this Work have been asserted
in accordance with the Copyright, Designs and Patents Act, 1988.

A CIP catalogue record for this book is available
from the British Library.

ISBN 978 1 4451 0177 4 (hbk)
ISBN 978 1 4451 0183 5 (pbk)

Series Editor: Melanie Palmer
Series Advisor: Catherine Glavina
Series Designer: Peter Scoulding

Printed in China

Franklin Watts is a division of
Hachette Children's Books,
an Hachette UK company
www.hachette.co.uk

Mum put out three

bowls of cornflakes.

"Let's go for a walk before breakfast," she said.

Brownilocks the bear was out walking, too. She smelt the cornflakes. "M-m-m, tasty," she thought, clambering in.

Brownilocks sat
on Dad's chair.
"Too hard!"
she growled.

So she tried
Mum's chair.
"Too soft!"
she moaned.

She went over to Sam's chair.
"Just right!" she thought,
reaching for Sam's cornflakes.

But ... CRASH!
Brownilocks was too
heavy and Sam's
chair snapped.

Brownilocks felt sleepy. She tried the biggest bed. "Too hard!" she grunted.

She tried the next bed. "Too bouncy!" she cried.

Then she tried the smallest bed.
"Just right!" she said, so she
climbed on and fell
fast asleep.

Mum, Dad and Sam came back from their walk. Dad frowned. "Who's been sitting in my chair?" he asked.

"Who's been sitting in my chair?"
Mum gasped. But Sam yelled,
"Who's broken my chair and
eaten all my cornflakes?"

They looked all over the house.

"Who's been sleeping in our bed?" cried Dad.

"And in this bed!" cried Mum.

"Hey! Look who's in my bed!"
yelled Sam. "And she's snoring!"

Brownilocks woke up,
ran downstairs and
outside. She ran across the
garden and into the woods.

"She was a nice bear,"
Sam sighed.
"I wish she'd come back."

Dad mended Sam's chair
and found a bean bag
for Brownilocks.

Next morning, Mum put out four
bowls of cornflakes – one for her,
one for Sam, one for Dad and
a big one for the bear.

Brownilocks soon came back
when she smelt the cornflakes.

"Here's your bowl," said Sam.

"Here's your bean bag," called Dad.

Brownilocks sat on Dad's chair.

"Try the bean bag," Dad said.

Brownilocks tried Sam's bowl.

"This one's bigger!"

said Sam.

Brownilocks scoffed up all the cornflakes and slurped up all the milk.

Brownilocks yawned. She thumped up the stairs and lay on Sam's bed.

Then Sam curled up with
Brownilocks and read her a story.

But Brownilocks longed to be
outside. She climbed out of
the window and ran
into the woods.

Sam wanted to see his new friend again. "Come back soon!" he cried.

Brownilocks liked the woods, but she also liked Sam – and the tasty cornflakes.

She did come back the very next day, and the day after that, and the day after that!

Puzzle 1

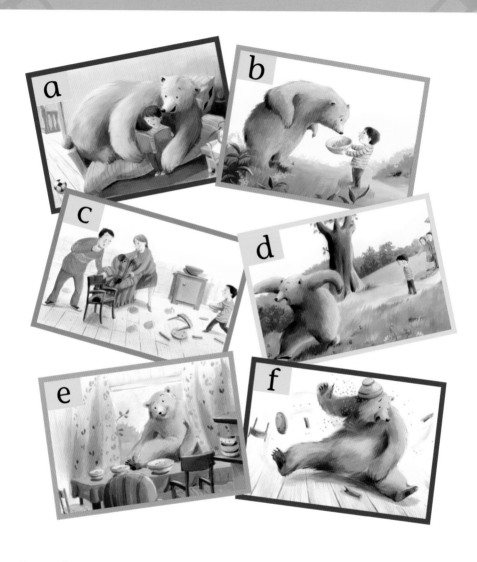

Put these pictures in the correct order.
Which event do you think is most important?
Now try writing the story in your own words!

Puzzle 2

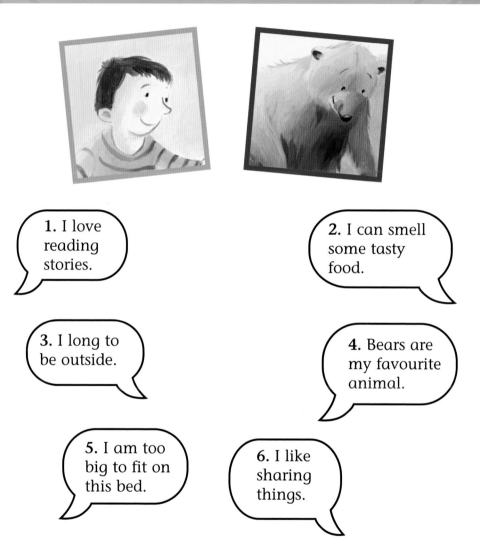

1. I love reading stories.

2. I can smell some tasty food.

3. I long to be outside.

4. Bears are my favourite animal.

5. I am too big to fit on this bed.

6. I like sharing things.

Choose the correct speech bubbles for each character. Can you think of any others? Turn over to find the answers.

Answers

Puzzle 1

The correct order is: 1e, 2f, 3c, 4d, 5a, 6b

Puzzle 2

Sam: 1, 4, 6

Brownilocks: 2, 3, 5
